Little Orange Honey Hood

Young
Palmetto
Books

Kim Shealy Jeffcoat,
Series Editor

Little Orange Honey Hood

A CAROLINA FOLKTALE

Lisa Anne Cullen

The University of South Carolina Press

For Jeff, Mom, Grandma, and Mary

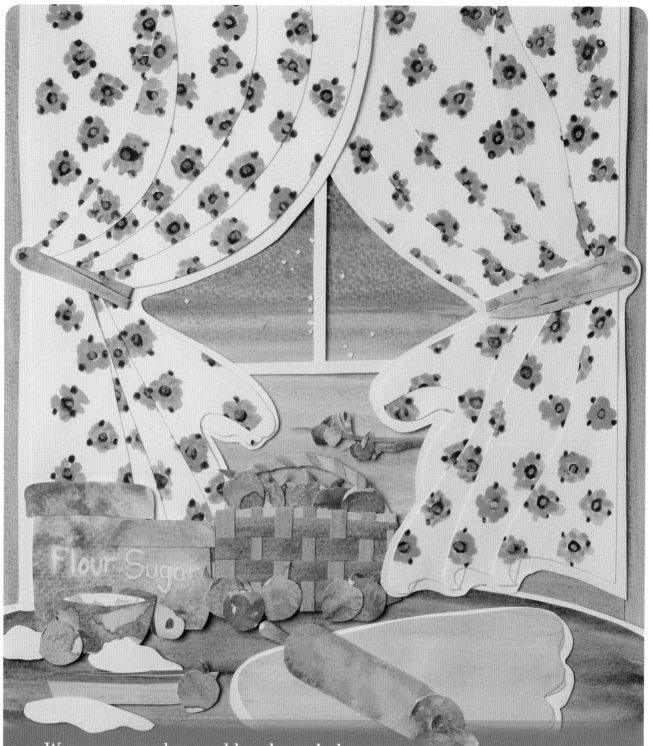

Warm summer breezes blew through the cottage windows and scattered Mama's flour from the kitchen tabletop to the floor.

"Blossom," Mama called out.

"Yes, Mama." Blossom's voice purred like a whip-poor-will on a star-studded night.

"I'm making a peach pie for Grandma," Mama said. She flattened the crust with her rolling pin. "I want you to take it to her in the morning."

"Alone?" Blossom asked.
"Yes. You're old enough," Mama said.
"Can I take the boat?" Blossom asked.
"I'll be taking the boat to Grandma's," said Mama.
"You'll have to take the trail."
"The trail is so long," said Blossom.

"Grandma needs her medicine," said Mama. "She's got mosquito fever and feeling a little green. This peach pie, orange-blossom honey, and black tea will heal her ailing. I'll catch up with you at Grandma's before supper. Now go on up to bed. When you close your eyes, carry the soothing bellows of the bullfrogs into your dreams."

"Into my dreams . . . ," Blossom sang out. She rushed to her room. On tip-toes, she reached into her closet, then hung her orange traveling cloak over her rocking chair.

She patted the delicate wrinkles, then hopped into bed next to the open window. The moonbeams danced upon the marsh, and the night song of the river carried Blossom into a deep sleep.

Just before sunrise, Blossom sprang out of bed, got dressed, and whirled her thin orange cloak over her shoulders. She tucked her hair into the hood, fastened the acorn button, and twirled like a tangerine twisting off a tree.

On the table next to the front door, Blossom found Mama's palmetto basket. Tucked inside was Grandma's medicine—peach pie, orange-blossom honey, and black tea. Atop the basket was Mama's pie cutter and a note. Blossom pulled back the curtain to let the orange sun shine a light. Blossom whispered, careful not to wake Mama.

Dear Blossom,
Be safe, sweet girl.
Walk the sunny trail.
Don't talk to strangers.
Use my pie cutter for
Grandma's peach pie.
I love you,
Mama xo

Next to the basket was Blossom's breakfast—a sugar-crusted blackberry muffin. Blossom gobbled it up before her shoes soaked up the morning dew.

She headed down the trail toward the plump orange sun. The river wind barely whispered at dawn. The marsh water lay as flat as a pancake, the cattail reeds stood soldier-tall, and one lonely cricket ratcheted his legs at the base of a pine. The rest of the crickets were asleep, plumb tired from strumming all night.

Blossom approached the edge of the river. She stood next to their boat. Cool mist rising from the water ran goose-bumps up her arms and tickled her earlobes.

A vine of Carolina jessamine blossomed at the base of a cypress tree just out of Blossom's reach. Jessamine was Grandma's favorite flower. Blossom stepped through thick palmetto to grab it. A sudden splash of swamp water soaked her orange cloak as an alligator jumped through the cattails onto shore.

"What 'cha doing, little girl?" he asked. His breath smelled like old spinach.

Blossom's heart beat hard. "I'm visiting my grandma upriver. She's got mosquito fever." Blossom jumped up, straightened her damp orange cloak, gripped her basket tight, and walked toward the trail. "You, Mr. Alligator, are a stranger. And I don't talk to strangers."

Alligator eyed Grandma's dock, then slipped into the river and disappeared into the muddy brown waters.

Blossom headed up the trail toward Grandma's house, jumping over cypress knees and fallen pines. "I'm coming, Grandma," she panted as she ran.

Grandma woke to a KNOCK, KNOCK, KNOCK
at her door.
"Who is it?" she hollered from bed.
Alligator said, "It's me, Grandma. It's me."

"Blossom? Well, crazy cattails, child. Come on in." Grandma looked through the thick mosquito net surrounding her bed.

Alligator pushed the door open with his long nose. The door creaked like a swarm of noon crickets.

"Blossom, I said 'come in,'" Grandma said.

"I'm right here, Grandma," said Alligator. He slammed the door shut with his swamp-wet tail, slipped under the mosquito net and bed covers, and swallowed Grandma whole. She slid down his throat like a slurped oyster off its shell. Alligator flossed his teeth with her orange hair ribbon. He then tied the ribbon into a bow on his bumpy green head and fell into a deep sleep in Grandma's cozy feather bed.

Waves of cricket calls followed Blossom up the trail. She KNOCK, KNOCK, KNOCKED on Grandma's door. Her orange cloak was drenched with sweat. In a low, mossy voice Alligator said, "Come in."

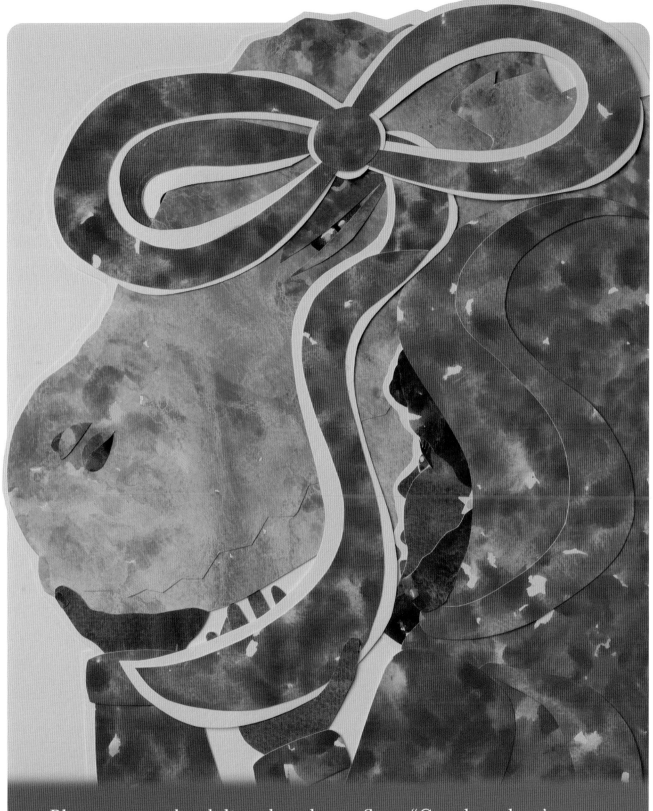

Blossom entered and slipped on the wet floor. "Grandma, there's swamp water under my feet." She set her palmetto basket on the bedside table and parted the mosquito net. "Oh my, Grandma!" Blossom said. "Mama said you were feeling a little green, but oh, my! That must have been one mean mosquito that bit you. You have a *very* serious swamp flu, Grandma."

"So," asked Alligator, "what do you have there?"
Blossom reached into the basket. "Your
medicine, Grandma."

"Yum," said Alligator. "Dessert." Alligator
grabbed his round stomach and burped. The thick
air smelled like a mix of old spinach and lavender.

"I've never heard you burp, Grandma." Blossom pinched her nose.
"Grandma, why is your breath so bad?"

"I swallowed the mosquito that bit me and he's stuck in my throat," said
Alligator. "Do you want to see?" he asked.

"No," said Blossom.

Alligator tapped his teeth with his long, sharp nails.

"Grandma, why are your nails so long and sharp?"

"So I can reach that mosquito bite," said Alligator. "Will you come closer and scratch it for me?"

Blossom knew that Grandma never burped, and she never burped bad breath. She never ate mosquitoes. And she never scratched her mosquito bites, ever. Blossom squinted her eyes at Grandma. She clenched her teeth and took a big step closer to Grandma's bed. "Sure, Grandma, I'll scratch your back. Turn over so I can reach it for you."

Alligator grinned a jagged-toothy grin,
fluffed Grandma's pillows, and lay on his full,
round belly.

"Grandma," Blossom said while she
scratched Alligator's rough, bumpy back, "your
hair ribbon is a little crooked."

Blossom yanked on the hair ribbon, and, as
fast as lightning, wrapped it around his snout!

Alligator lunged at her.

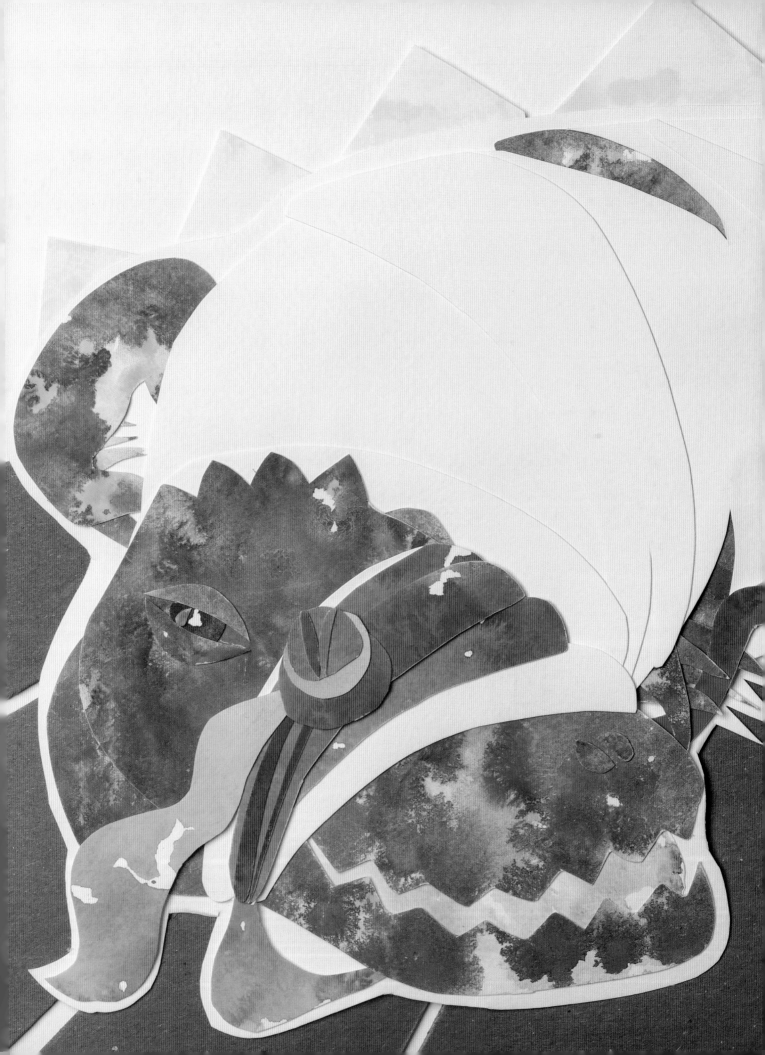

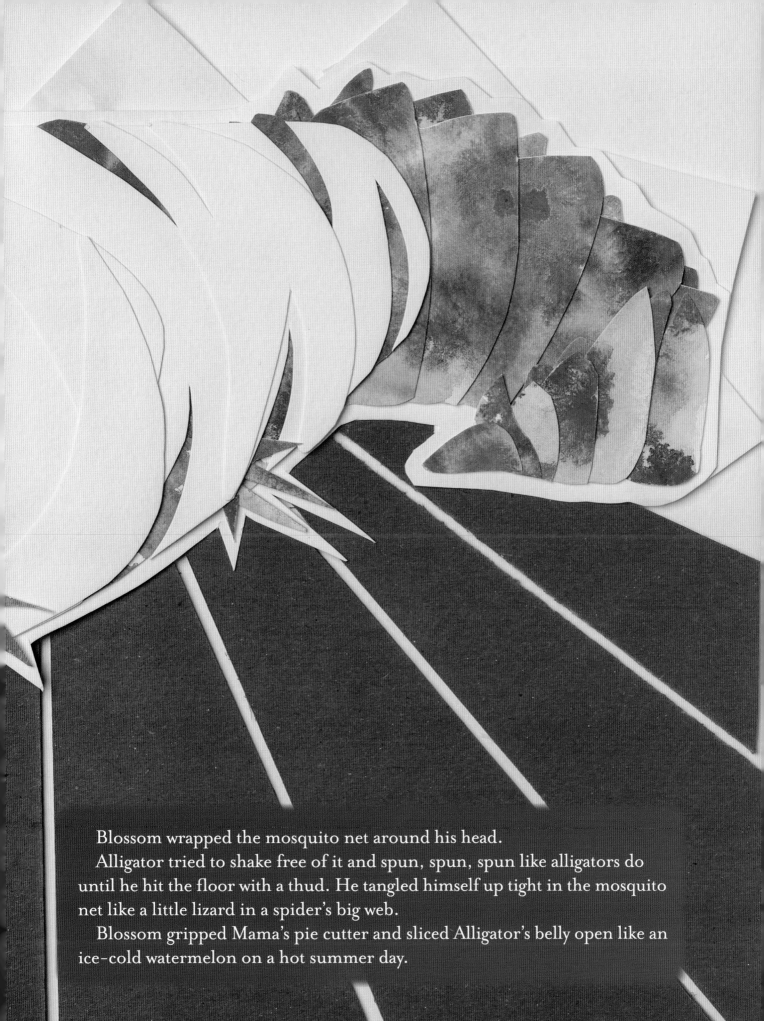

Blossom wrapped the mosquito net around his head.

Alligator tried to shake free of it and spun, spun, spun like alligators do until he hit the floor with a thud. He tangled himself up tight in the mosquito net like a little lizard in a spider's big web.

Blossom gripped Mama's pie cutter and sliced Alligator's belly open like an ice-cold watermelon on a hot summer day.

Grandma popped out!
"Well, crazy cattails, Blossom," Grandma said, "you
are a golden ray of Carolina sunshine. And, pee-yew,
I smell like swamp muck. Would you fill the tub for me,
child? I'd like to take a cool bubble bath."

After her bubble bath, Grandma donned fresh orange pajamas and showered Blossom with lavender hugs and kisses.

Blossom tucked Grandma into a freshly made bed, then flipped through the pages of Grandma's cookbooks.

Blossom stirred up her first-ever summertime river feast. Honey-grilled gator tail, deep fried gator nuggets, and piping hot, sweet-sugar corn bread filled Grandma's cottage with luscious aromas.

Then, Blossom stitched a new gator-hide hair ribbon for Grandma and tied it into her fluffy white hair.

As the sun melted into the marsh, just as the table was set, Mama rowed the boat up to Grandma's dock. Mama carried fresh-picked Carolina jessamine and plunked it into a wooden vase at the center of the table.

After dinner they all sipped hot, black tea drizzled with orange-blossom honey, and they ate tart-sweet peach pie until their plump bellies jiggled as they giggled into the night.

Grandma's mosquito fever was gone before the moonbeams danced upon the marsh. Mama, Blossom, and Grandma fell fast asleep. They snored little snores in harmony with the cricket-frog symphony floating on the warm summer breezes outside.

North Carolina and South Carolina State Symbols

Date Adopted	State	Type	Symbol
1924	South Carolina	Flower	Yellow Jessamine
1939	South Carolina	Tree	Sabal Palmetto
1963	North Carolina	Tree	Pine
1973	North Carolina	Insect	Honeybee
1984	South Carolina	Fruit	Peach
1987	North Carolina	Boat	Shad Boat

Source: http://www.statesymbolsusa.org/

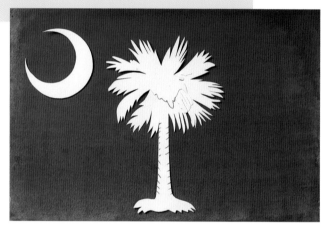

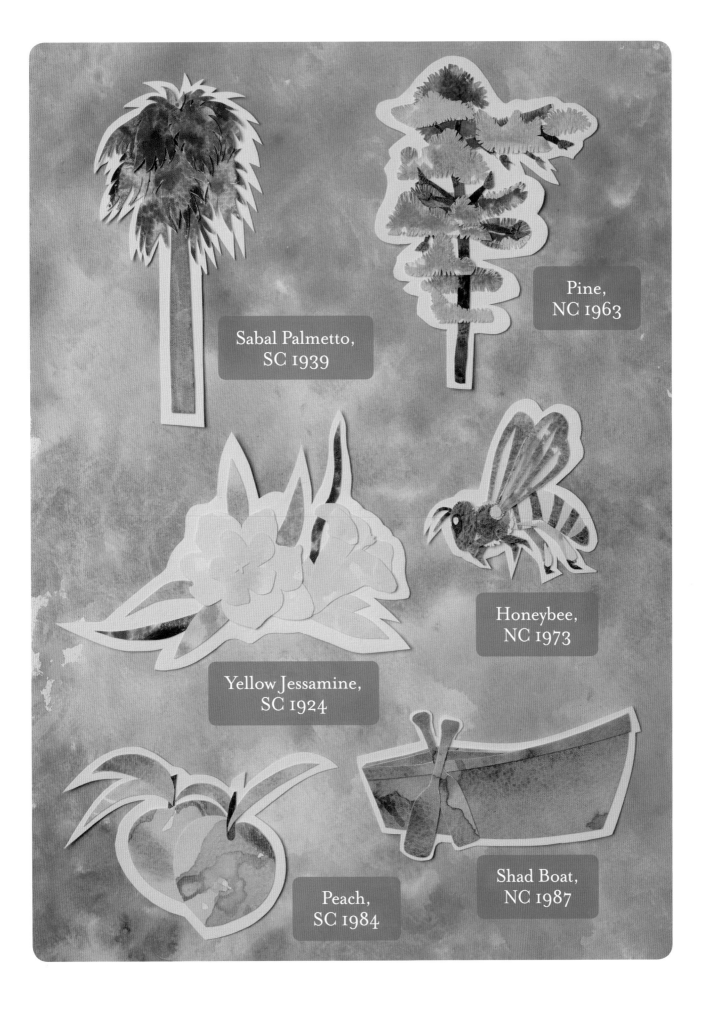

Sabal Palmetto,
SC 1939

Pine,
NC 1963

Yellow Jessamine,
SC 1924

Honeybee,
NC 1973

Peach,
SC 1984

Shad Boat,
NC 1987

The following recipes are to be used with adult supervision.

Black Tea with Honey

8 black tea bags
Orange-blossom honey
8 cups water
8 tea cups or coffee mugs

Boil water. Remove pot from heat. Place all 8 tea bags into hot pot. Let tea bags set in water for 15 minutes. Stir occasionally. Remove tea bags. Pour tea in cups, add desired amount of honey, and add cream or milk, which is optional. Enjoy.

Peach Pie

8 Carolina peaches
1 fresh lemon
½ cup sugar
½ teaspoon salt
3 tablespoons cornstarch
2 pie pastries for a top crust and
    bottom crust

Preheat oven to 375°. Peel and slice the peaches. Squeeze the lemon juice over the peach slices, stir, and set aside. In a separate bowl mix the sugar, salt, and cornstarch. Combine all ingredients together. Place one pie pastry in the bottom of the pie tin. Pour in the peach pie filling. Place the second pie pastry atop the pie, pinch the pie crusts together around the edge of the pie tin, then cut small slits in the top crust. Place the pie in the oven for 50 minutes. Keep an eye on the pie crust. If the edges get too brown, cover them with foil. Once cooked, let the pie cool for at least two hours then serve with tea and honey.

Deep Fried Gator Nuggets

1 pound gator meat (cut into chunks)
2 teaspoons salt
2 teaspoons pepper
2 cups flour
1 cup buttermilk

Place cut gator chunks into bowl. Add salt and pepper to meat and stir until all chunks are coated. Dip each chunk of meat into buttermilk, then roll each chunk of meat into the flour until coated completely. Deep fry chunks until cooked. Serve with hot sauce and blue cheese dressing.

Honey-Grilled Gator Tail

1 pound gator meat (cut into slices)
1 teaspoon salt
1 teaspoon pepper
1 tablespoon brown sugar
1 tablespoon honey
2 tablespoons soy sauce
¼ cup orange juice

Place cut gator slices into a bowl. Add salt and pepper to meat and stir until all slices are coated. In a separate bowl stir brown sugar, honey, soy sauce, and orange juice. Add sauce mixture to meat and let set for 2 hours in the refrigerator. Heat oven to 400°. Bake gator meat in an oven-safe pan for at least one hour, making sure to flip meat occasionally while cooking.

Sweet Sugar Corn Bread

1 cup flour
1 cup yellow cornmeal
½ cup sugar
1 teaspoon salt
3½ teaspoons baking powder
1 egg
1 cup milk
⅓ cup vegetable oil

Preheat oven to 400°. Spray or grease a 9-inch pan. In a large bowl, combine all ingredients. Pour batter into pan and sprinkle the top with a little extra sugar. Bake for 25 minutes or until golden brown and cooked through.

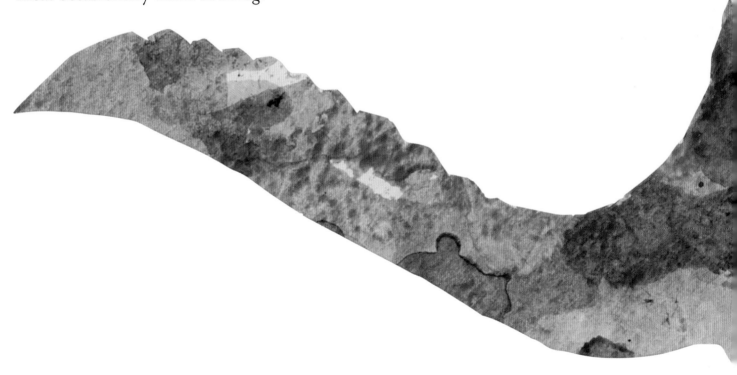

Published by the University of South Carolina Press
Columbia, South Carolina 29208

www.sc.edu/uscpress

Manufactured in China

27 26 25 24 23 22 21 20 19 18
10 9 8 7 6 5 4 3 2 1

Library of Congress Cataloging-in-Publication Data
can be found at http://catalog.loc.gov/.

ISBN: 978-1-61117-847-0 (hardcover)
ISBN: 978-1-61117-848-7 (ebook)